comets

The Tornado

S. B. V. Moody

Illustrated by
Clinton Banbury

CollinsEducational
An imprint of HarperCollins*Publishers*

Published by Collins Educational
77-85 Fulham Palace Road, London W6 8JB

© HarperCollins*Publishers*

ISBN 0 00 323064 3

Illustration, page layout and cover illustration by Clinton Banbury.
Cover design by Clinton Banbury.

Commissioning Editor: Domenica de Rosa
Editor: Paula Hammond
Production: Susan Cashin

Typeset by Jordan Publishing Design
Printed by Caledonian International, Glasgow, Scotland

The Tornado

Contents

Chapter 1
The Heart of the Home

Eric scanned the hen house. He knew that he had to find all the stray eggs. If his father found even one egg wedged in a corner or hidden under the straw, there would be trouble. No excuses. Just trouble.

The day had started badly. Eric's father had woken him up at dawn and told him to get to the hen house and gather the eggs.

Jump to it boy. Now! Storm's a brewing, and we've got to be ready.

Eric obeyed. He always obeyed but he hated it when his father ordered him around. He hated the stinging slaps, and the cold stares, especially the stares. They made him feel stupid, and worthless.

His mother had not made him feel that way. She even helped him understand his father better.

Only three eggs, hardly enough for me, let alone the rest of the family.

Even worse, no chicks would ever get to hatch. All the eggs would be needed for food.

When he was younger, he had taken care of the rooster and the chickens for his mother. Even now, he liked watching the hens sitting on their eggs.

Jump, jump, jump. Gotta jump,
if you want to get along.

He was 15 now,
almost a man. He was tired
of jumping at his father's commands,
and he didn't like thinking about his mother either.

4

His mother had been the gentle one, the buffer between him and his father. Now she was gone, whisked away when he was at school by the tornado that had flattened the old family farm house. She had left three children. Eric was the oldest and Sarah the youngest.

If he closed his eyes, he could remember her.

Remember Eric, you are the heart of the home.

But now he was ready to break out from home, like a chick from an egg. But he knew he'd need more than a chick's egg tooth to do it. He had to face his father first. Where was Pa, anyway? He couldn't be out in the fields, with the storm on its way.

He finally found his father in the tool shed working on their ancient pick-up truck. He was having trouble because the jack kept slipping.

Eggs are collected, Pa. Want me to fix breakfast?

Get your sister to do it. You check the animals. Get 'em some feed, but don't let none of them out. You hear?

8

Even though Lizzy was only six, she tried hard to act like a mother, especially when it came to loving her cat.

The wind was picking up now. Cyclones of dust whipped across the yard. Storms were always scary on the Kansas plains.

One minute, **Eric** and Sarah were happily loading up the haycart, the next, a streak of lightning seemed to rise from the old Cottonwood tree. The tree exploded as if it had been stuffed with dynamite. Branches flew across the yard, the massive tree trunk loomed over Sarah and the cart.

But could they get it hooked up in time to save the barn?
And what about the animals? What about his horse,
Tomahawk?

Then Eric had an idea…

Horses. Trough. Water. Blanket.

The horse trough was full of water. He had just filled it. That was what he needed. Water and blankets.

They all worked together. Plunging blankets and feed sacks deep into the trough. Eric's muscles ached. His breath came in ragged gasps.

Chapter 3
THE STORM CELLAR

He had to get to the storm cellar. That was what Pa had said. The cellar was not much more than a deep tunnel in the ground, near where their farm house had once stood. It was the best place to be in a storm.

Eric and Sarah huddled together in the cellar.

It's too dark. I'm scared.

The banging of the cellar doors grew louder as the wind heaved them apart and smashed them against the ground. Eric knew he should close them, but where was Lizzy? Where was Pa?

Questions raced through Eric's mind.

What if Pa and Lizzy were trapped inside the trailer and
a tornado was coming? 'Don't leave for nothing' his
father had ordered, and Eric always did what his father
said. 'But this isn't nothing,' Eric told himself. 'This is
Lizzy. This is Pa.'

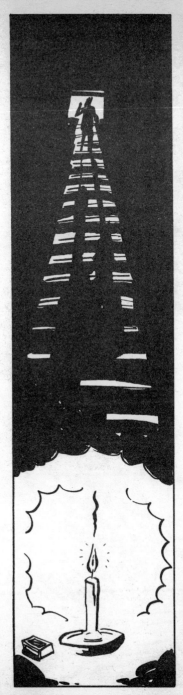

Lizzy was standing barefoot in the dust.

LIZZY! GET IN THE SHELTER!

BUT PA'S OUT HERE! PA AND TABBY. BUT I DON'T KNOW WHERE.

Suddenly, there was silence. The wind had stopped, like a giant fan being turned off.

Thank goodness! It's stopped. Now we can find them

Chapter 4

The Tornado

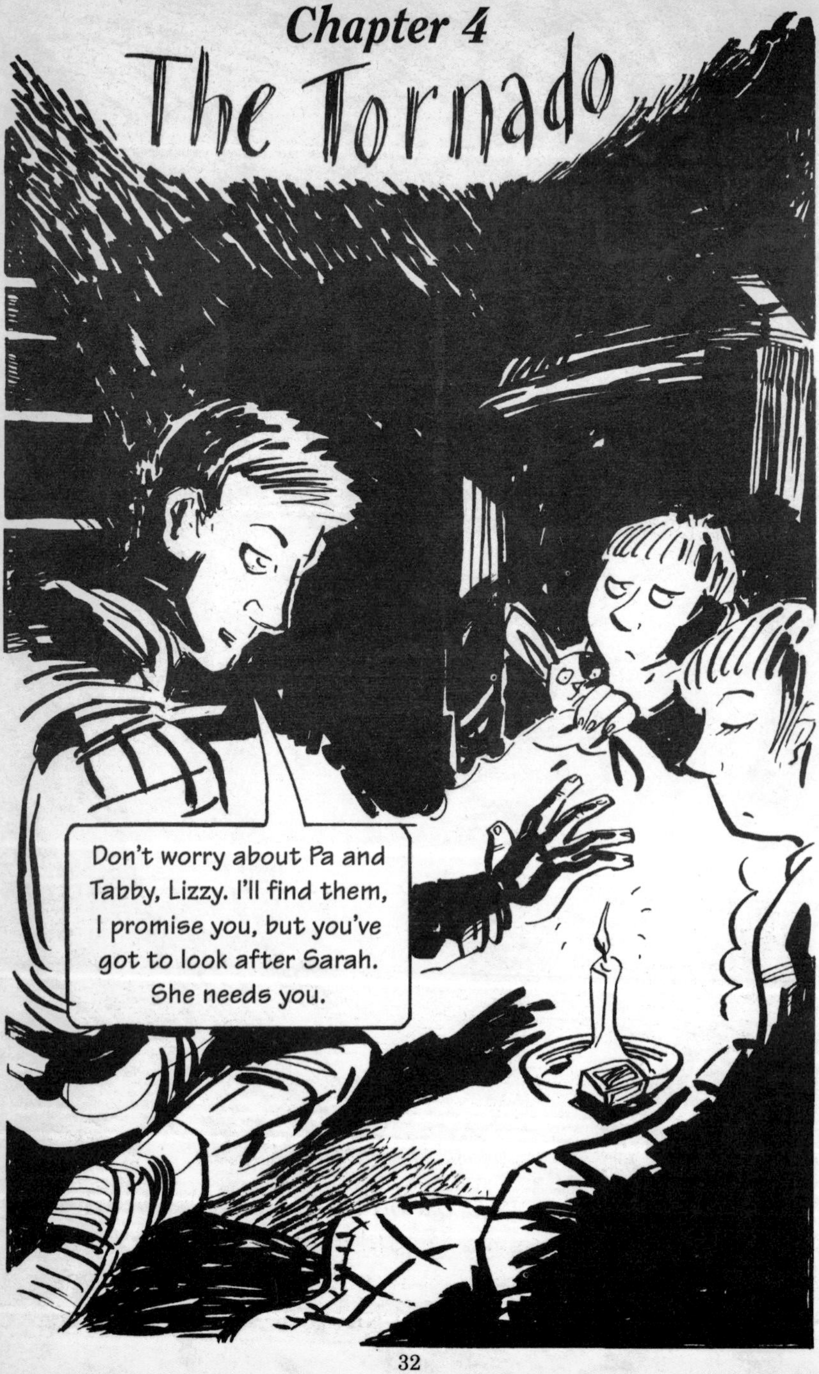

It was just like he knew it would be. A black funnel in the sky, tearing into the earth. Would it pass the farm by or would it go straight though it like it did when mom was killed? He didn't know. He just knew he had to find Pa.

Why didn't his father answer?

The wind was
even stronger now.
He had to shield his
eyes to see. No Pa. No Tabby.
There was only dirt and the
funnel cloud, looming black in the
distance like a giant vacuum cleaner,
sucking up everything in its path.

There were only two places left to look, the barn and the tool shed. Would there be time to search both?

At least he could set the animals free. They would probably have a better chance loose in the fields than tied up in their stalls.

There was only one place left to search.

He squeezed under the truck. His father's foot was trapped near his ankle, pinned by the flat tyre and the weight of the truck.

He had to try to lift the truck but would
the jack hold this time?

The tornado was nearer. It had grown massive, gorging on everything in its path and thundering and roaring like an out-of-control train. Eric knew that if the funnel came their way, they were in trouble. Tornadoes could snatch you up and spit you out in seconds. And in those seconds a farm could be destroyed and lives could be lost.

Frantically he pumped the jack, but the lever wouldn't hold. It kept slipping and the jack had only raised the truck a few inches. He could be injuring his father's foot even more, and the tornado was getting closer. Thunderclaps shook the ground, exploding like fireworks.

Using all his strength, Eric dragged the branch towards the tool-shed.

He wedged the branch under the wheel then began to pump the jack, up and down, up and down. Inch by inch, the jack lifted the truck. The wind whipped his hair and stung his eyes. Lightning made him jump in terror but he kept pumping, willing the tornado to stay away.